I FEEL ORANGE TODAY

Story by Patricia Godwin
Art by Kitty Macaulay

ANNICK PRESS LTD., TORONTO, CANADA

Second Printing, October 1993

Annick Press Ltd.

Annick Press gratefully acknowledges the support of the Canada
Council and the Ontario Arts Council.

Canadian Cataloguing in Publication Data

Godwin, patriciaJ.
 I feel orange today

Poems.
ISBN 1-55037-284-X (bound) ISBN 1-55037-285-8 (pbk.)

1.Macaulay, Kitty. I. Title.

PS8563.G3153 1993   jC811'54   C92-094636-4
PZ8.3.G63 If 1993

The art in this book was rendered in watercolour, pen and ink.
The text was typeset in Goudy by Attic Typesetting.

Distributed in Canada by:
Firefly Books Ltd.
250 Sparks Ave.
Willowdale, ON M2H 2S4

Published in the USA by Annick Press (U.S.) Ltd.
Distributed in the U.S.A. by:
Firefly Books Ltd.
P.O. Box 1325
Ellicott Station
Buffalo, NY 14205

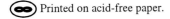 Printed on acid-free paper.

Printed and bound in Canada by
D.W. Friesen & Sons, Altona, Manitoba.

To Dylan and Jesse and the
memory of their grandmother
Kathleen
P.G.

To Moo-Moo, *The Big Fish*,
and Baby Rabbit
K.M.

I feel orange today. Orange is
        sitting at the beach, hot and salty,

with juice-sticky fingers,
    waiting to go swimming.

Grey days are slow. I don't want to think or do anything. Misty, my cat, knows what a grey day is. She looks like one.

Blue is a cool day,
water, blueberry popsicles,
shadows when we're camping.
Some people say blue means sad
but not to me.

I like yellow days.
Mr. Sun lights up all the corners
of my secret fort.
Joel, my best friend, plays with me
all day.

Black isn't a day.
Black is a night,
stretching far away
with no end.
When I think
of black
thunderclouds,
blowing like witches' hair,
I feel small
but happy because
they are so
beautiful.

Today is a green day. The world is quiet
except for the rustling of leaves.

The tree-cooled breeze brushes my arm
   while I watch a busy ant in the grass.

Red days tire me out.
A red day is when you call the teacher
Mom by mistake
or you get mad at your brother
or sometimes just at yourself.

White days make me feel like doing things. On the first day of school, I want to write on the new white pages of my books.

When it snows, I want to be the first one to put footprints in it. When I put on my white shirt and tie, I know something exciting is going to happen.

Purple days
are a muddle.
Sometimes I feel
bright blazing purple.
Sometimes I feel gentle sad violet.
I don't know where
I lost my shoes
and it wasn't me that left the light on.

Sometimes I feel a little bit like
all the colours.
Come to think of it,
most days are really a rainbow.